BENEATH COLD WATERS
The Marine Life of New England

Frilled Sea Anemones and a Northern Basket Star, *Metridium senile* and *Gorgonocephalus arcticus*.

BENEATH COLD WATERS
The Marine Life of New England

FRED BAVENDAM

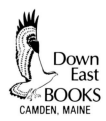

Down East BOOKS
CAMDEN, MAINE

To my parents

Library of Congress Catalog
Card Number 79-67413
ISBN 0-89272-184-7

4

4 5 3

Contents

Foreword & Notes

THIS BOOK IS INSPIRED by the many people who ask me, "What's down there?" as I come ashore after a dive. Television specials and many books have shown the beauty of the sea, but for the most part New England's waters have been bypassed in favor of tropical seas and coral reefs. The purpose of this book is to show the wealth of marine life in New England's cold waters.

The reader should be aware that the animals shown here are only a small sampling. Over three hundred different fish have been recorded in the Gulf of Maine. The invertebrate species found there number in the thousands. Those shown here are among the most common.

I have tried to show each animal in its natural surroundings. This precludes a great number of invertebrates, such as clams and worms, which burrow beneath the surface of the ocean's floor. Many animals are too small to photograph adequately while in the ocean. Numerous fish are shy enough or fast enough to elude my cameras.

Despite these shortcomings, I feel this book fills the need for a book of photographs, rather than drawings. For those interested in more detailed investigations, several books are especially worthwhile. *A Field Guide to the Atlantic Seashore* by Kenneth Gosner is an especially worthwhile book on the invertebrates. *Fishes of the Gulf of Maine* by Henry Bigelow and William Schroeder is the best reference for the fish. And *The Gulf of Maine* by Spencer Apollonio covers the oceanography of the Gulf of Maine.

Northern Red Anemone and Stalked Ascidians, *Tealia felina* and *Boltenia ovifera.*

I would also like to express my thanks to the many people who have helped and encouraged me in this endeavor. A number of the members of the Zoology Department at the University of New Hampshire were helpful as I struggled to identify the animals I had photographed. I would especially like to thank Lorus and Margery Milne, Larry Harris, Terry Gosliner, Barry Spracklin, Paul Langer, Wendell Brown, Alan Waterfield, Charles Walker, and Butch Huntley.

Northern Basket Star and a Deep Sea Scallop, *Gorgonocephalus arcticus* and *Placopecten magellanicus.*

THE GULF OF MAINE

THE GULF OF MAINE is a large, cold backwater of the North Atlantic. It is bounded on the south by the long arm of Cape Cod. Its western edge follows the shoreline northward along the coasts of northern Massachusetts, New Hampshire, Maine, and parts of New Brunswick and Nova Scotia. Almost two hundred miles to the east, its seaward rim is formed by the shallows of Nantucket Shoals, Georges Bank, and Browns Bank. This forms a roughly rectangular body of water covering about 36,000 square miles with an average depth of almost 500 feet. The greatest depth, found in Georges Basin, is 1,236 feet. Near this deep basin is the Northeast Channel, the only deepwater passage from the Gulf of Maine into the Atlantic.

The broad banks, renowned for their rich fishing, are so shallow as to nearly seal the Gulf of Maine from outside water circulation. Small amounts of colder water do enter the gulf across the Scotian Shelf, but this is somewhat offset by warmer water from the continental shelf entering through the Northeast Channel. So, in fact, the cold water temperatures are reflections of the New England climate.

Within the Gulf of Maine itself there is a counter-clockwise flow of the surface waters. This is strongest in the spring when it is reinforced by the heavy runoff of freshwater from the rivers. There is also a diurnal, twice daily, tidal flow within the Gulf. This is strongest in the northeast quarter of the gulf where the Bay of Fundy

LEFT   Ribbon Kelp, *Laminaria saccharina.*

has some of the strongest tides in the world, averaging 36 feet in height.

The area within the Gulf of Maine is part of a biogeographical area known as the *American Atlantic Boreal Region.* This region begins on the north side of Cape Cod and extends northward to Labrador. The broad community of plants and animals that characterize a major habitat is called a biome. The rocky coast of the Gulf of Maine is a marine biome called the *Balanoid-Thallophyte Biome.* This community of organisms is typified by large numbers of barnacles and dense aquatic vegetation. There is a well defined succession of different organisms as one moves downward through the intertidal zone, starting with barnacles, then blue mussels, followed by several types of seaweed.

Sub-tidally, the *Balanoid-Thallophyte Biome,* is inhabited by a wide variety of invertebrates and fish. Many of the invertebrates are sessile, anchored to the bottom where they feed on what the currents bring them. These include many species of bivalve mollusks, coelenterates, and tunicates. There are also many animals that roam the bottom in search of food. Among them are many crustaceans, snails, and bottom fish.

Further out from shore is the *Pelagic Biome,* the home of the plants and animals that drift or swim in the open waters. This includes the microscopic plants, called phytoplankton, that are the primary producers of the oceans and form the basis for the food chains. Common Gulf of Maine phytoplankton include diatoms, radiolarians, desmids, and dinoflagellates. These are eaten by tiny animals called zooplankton, which are eaten by still larger zooplankton, which in turn are eaten by larger invertebrates and fish. The zooplankton population of the Gulf of Maine is so dominated by copepods of the genus Calanus, that it is described as a Calanus Community. The Calanus community includes amphipods, chaetognaths, pteraopods, ctenophores, and many others.

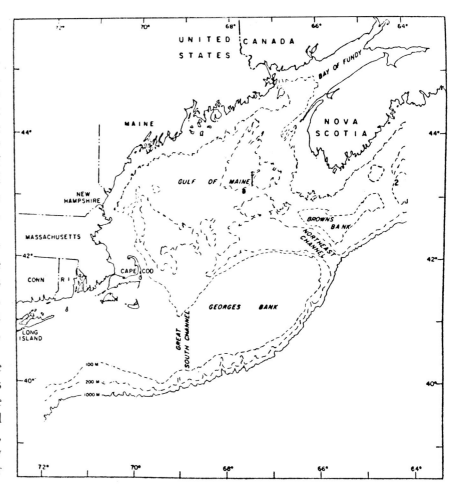

There are definite seasonal variations in the species and numbers of plankton. Mid-winter marks the low point in the plankton populations. In late February or early March there is a vast bloom in the phytoplankton called diatoms. This begins in the southern coastal region of the Gulf of Maine and spreads northward and seaward. This is followed by an increase of the zooplankton which feed on them. By early summer the diatoms have greatly diminished and phytoplankton called Peridinians dominate. As the summer progresses, the zooplankton slowly reduce the numbers of phytoplankton. In the fall there is usually a final phytoplankton bloom before the days grow shorter and all the plankton decline to winter levels.

Inshore, the pelagic plankton are often outnumbered by the vast hatches of planktonic larvae of many of the invertebrates, especially during the late spring and early summer.

Cape Cod is not just a physical boundary, but a biological one as well. Water temperatures on the north and south sides of the Cape often differ by as much as ten degrees Fahrenheit. Many warm water animals drift or swim northward in the heat of the summer to the south side of Cape Cod, but few of these enter the Gulf of Maine and survive. A true indicator of the effectiveness of this barrier is the fact that while 60% to 80% of the species of seaweeds and animals indigenous to the Gulf of Maine are found in Northern Europe, only 7% to 8% of the animals from south of the Cape are shared. The Gulf of Maine is truely New England's waters and the animals found there are New England's marine life.

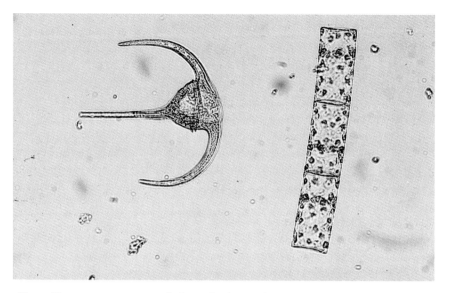

TOP   Two common types of phytoplankton, shown magnified about three hundred times, are cylindrical desmids and a horned dinoflagellate.

BOTTOM   A Calanoid Copepod, shown magnified about seventy times.

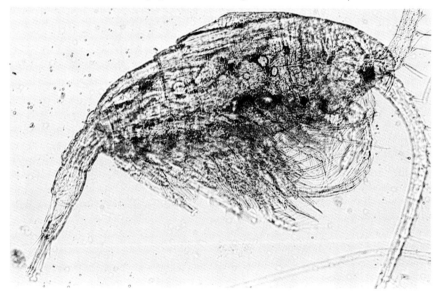

Frilled Sea Anemone, *Metridium senile.*

NOMENCLATURE

TODAY, well over a million different animals have been recorded and identified. Each year new animals are discovered, many of them from the oceans of the world. The vast majority of these animals, known only to specialists in a particular field of study, have no common names and are known only by their scientific names. The method by which animals are given their scientific names is called the binomial system of nomenclature. This method was first proposed by the famous Swedish naturalist Linnaeus in 1758. Using this system, each animal is given a name consisting of two parts. The first part or name is the genera name and is always capitalized. A genera or genus is a small group of animals that share a great many characteristics. The second name is the species name and is not capitalized. This name distinguishes the animal from all similar animals. The two names together, usually set in italic print, identify the animal, as in the case of the rock crab, *Cancer irroratus*.

Over the years a systematic heirarchy has been adopted to put order into the plant and animal kingdoms. The animals have been divided into groups, sub-groups, and still smaller sub-groups in a manner that indicates shared characteristics and follows the supposed evolutionary lines. The major groupings are Phylum, Class, Order,

LEFT Purple Sea Star on Blue Mussels and Breadcrumb Sponge, *Asterias vulgaris* on *Mytilus edulis* and *Halichondria panicea*.

Family, Genus, and finally Species. In groups where the number of species is great, such as the Crustaceans, further divisions are used. Each name of a particular grouping identifies a characteristic of the animals in that group. For example, the rock crab, *Cancer irroratus*, belongs to the Order Decapoda within the Class Crustacea. This order identifies those crustaceans that have ten (deca) feet (poda).

Despite the world-wide acceptance of the binomial system of nomenclature, considerable confusion still exists on the names of many animals. In some cases naturalists in different parts of the world gave different names to the same animal without realizing they were in fact the same species. This was especially true many years ago. The sea star we call *Asterias vulgaris* is called *Asterias rubens* in Europe where it is also found. Another source of difficulty has been the fact that many marine animals grow through stages that bear little or no resemblance to the adult form. A great many marine animals have minute planktonic phases that aid in the dispersal and distribution of the species. Adding further to the confusion is the fact that some animals, like the hydromedusea in the Phylum Coelenterata, have alternating generations of sessile hydroid and planktonic medusae. Unaware that they were the same animal, naturalists gave each form a different name. The beautiful hydroid *Corymorpha pendula*, has a medusoid stage called *Steenstrupia rubra*.

In an effort to avoid further confusion, I have used both the common and scientific names adopted by Kenneth Gosner in his *Field Guide to the Atlantic Seashore*. In some cases I have been able to carry identification only down to the genus level, especially where microscopic examination is necessary to detect the distinctions between species. These animals are identified by the Genus name and the letters sp. referring to species. Therefore, in the case of the first of the sponge plates, Isodictya sp., the identification would be a sponge of the Genus Isodictya with the exact species undetermined.

SPONGES: Phylum Porifera

SPONGES ARE A GROUP of marine and freshwater sea-animals with world-wide distribution. They are found in every ocean and in shallow waters downward to depths of over a thousand feet. Adult sponges are usually attached to some solid substrate. There are many species of sponge in New England, but none of any commercial value.

Morphologically, sponges are among the simplest of the multi-celled animals. Early naturalists were once divided as to whether sponges were actually plants or animals. Today there is still some question as to whether a sponge is a single animal or a colony. Sponges have neither organs nor organ systems. They also have no power of locomotion. Sponges grow asexually, but sexual reproduction also occurs. The sexes are indistinguishable, but many sponges are hermaphroditic.

Sponges feed by filtering sea water through a network of canals in their bodies. The water is drawn into the sponge through minute pores called ostia. Inside the body of the sponge specialized cells

LEFT Palmate Sponges, *Isodictya sp.* This family of sponges is characterized by broad, thick branches with a stout base. It has large, easily visible oscula and often grows to over a foot in height.

OPPOSITE PAGE Eyed Finger Sponge, *Haliclona oculata.* The eyed finger sponge is a very common sponge that is found in both deep and shallow water. It is usually a straw brown in color and has smaller oscula than the palmate sponges. Clumps of this sponge may reach a foot and a half in height.

Eyed Finger Sponge, *Haliclona oculata*

Crumb of Bread Sponge, *Halichondria panicea*

Boring Sponge, *Cliona celata*

called collar cells filter out minute planktonic organisms and bits of detritus. The water is then expelled through larger pores called oscula.

The sponge gets its shape from a supporting skeleton composed of a network of needle-like spines called spicules or protein fibers called spongin. Some sponges have both. The spicules are composed of either calcium carbonate or silica.

Because both the shape and color of a sponge are quite variable, identification by appearance is unreliable. A particular sponge growing in shallow water where it is subject to wave action may be flat and encrusting, while another individual of the same species in deeper, calmer surroundings may have a taller branching shape. The common eyed-finger sponge occurs in a variety of colors: orange, yellow, brown or even lavender.

Positive identification requires microscopic examination of the spicules. A section of the sponge body can be dissolved in chlorine bleach leaving only the spicules. Then the spicules are examined to determine composition, shape, and size. Each sponge has a particular type of spicule or ratio of different type of spicules. This along with the external appearance allows accurate identification.

PRECEDING SPREAD LEFT   Crumb of Bread Sponge, *Halichondria panicea.* This sponge is typical of a number of the flat, encrusting sponges. It is abundant in shallow water just below the low tide mark. Colonies of this sponge may cover several square feet.

PRECEDING PAGE RIGHT   Boring Sponge, *Cliona celata.* This sponge bores holes in mollusk shells. As the infestation progresses it may overgrow the mollusk completely. It is important in the recycling of calcium in mollusk shells.

OPPOSITE PAGE   *Melonanchora elliptica.* Another encrusting sponge, Melonanchora has a surface with closely set wart-like papillae. It has a wide distribution on both sides of the Atlantic.

THIS PAGE TOP   *Polymastia robusta.* Polymastia sponges are usually found at depths of fifty feet or more in areas where rocky ledges give way to sand or mud. The many inch-long fingers grow up from a flat, spreading base that is often covered by sand or other sediments.

THIS PAGE BOTTOM   *Pellina sitiens.* This sponge is a relative of the Crumb of Bread Sponge. It is usually found in the colder waters of northern Maine or at depths below the thermocline. It may reach a size of several feet across.

Melonanchora elliptica

POLYPS AND MEDUSAE:
Phylum Cnidaria

THE CNIDARIANS ARE SOMETIMES CALLED the "flowers of the sea" despite the fact that they are animals and not plants. It is difficult to find any other group of marine animals that can equal their beauty.

The phylum includes such a wide variety of body shapes that it is difficult to make general statements about them. Most cnidarians exhibit radial symmetry around a simple gastrovascular cavity with a single opening, the mouth. Two basic body forms have evolved, one the polyp and the medusa.

The polyp, as typified by the sea anemone, is sessile. One end of its tubular body is attached to the substrate, while at the other end is the mouth surrounded by tentacles.

The medusea, as typified by jellyfish, is a swimming planktonic

LEFT   Nodding Nosegay Hydroid, *Corymorpha pendula.* This hydroid looks very much like an enlarged version of the Tubularian hydroids. It occurs as solitary individuals usually found on muddy bottoms in depths of about fifty feet. It grows up to four inches in height and has an alternating hydromedusoid stage.

OPPOSITE PAGE   Pink-hearted Hydroid, *Tubularia sp.* This is a very common hydroid in our waters. Colonial in nature, it often occurs in dense clumps resembling a bouquet of tiny, pink flowers. The hydroid polyp is about half an inch across. They are frequently found growing on pilings, jetties, and rocks from subtidal depths downward.

Pink-Hearted Hydroid, *Tubularia sp.*

ABOVE Snail Fur, *Hydrachtinia echinata*. This is an encrusting colony of hydroids that has the unusual characteristic of being parasitic and occuring only on mollusk shells that are inhabited by living hermit crabs. Only several sixteenths of an inch in height, the colony forms a pink fuzz on the hermit crab's shell.

RIGHT *Halecium sp.* This family of hydroids contains over a dozen similar species, many occurring in the Gulf of Maine. The feather-like branching colonies may reach a height of over six inches. These hydroids do not have a free-swimming medusoid stage.

form. It is generally bell-shaped with tentacles hanging from the margin. The mouth is situated on the underside.

Most cnidarians exhibit one body form or the other, but some have alternating generations of medusoid and polypoid stages. The phylum is divided into three classes; hydrozoa, scyphozoa, and anthozoa.

The hydrozoans are very numerous in New England waters. Most are quite small and delicate. Many of the hydrozoans have both a polyp stage called a hydroid, and a medusoid stage called a hydromedusa. Other hydrozoans have only one form or the other. Identification of the hydrozoans is often difficult and may require microscopic examination during the reproductive phase. Further complicating the nomenclature is the fact that early biologists were unaware of the connection between polyp and medusa stages and gave different names to each.

Obelia Hydroid, *Obelia sp.*, The Obelia hydroids are colonial animals and occur as numerous individuals on branching stems that grow to over an inch in height. They are frequently found as bushy white patches growing on the blades and stalks of the kelps. They have a hydromedusoid stage and are found abundantly throughout New England.

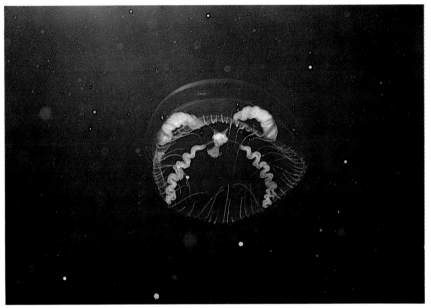

Mitrocomella polydiademata. This is one species of hydromedusae, which are the alternate stages of many hydroid polyps. They are frequently found in shallow water in the spring and summer. This species is about an inch across, but many species are smaller.

The scyphozoa are the larger more conspicuous jellyfish. In these cnidarians the medusoid stage is dominant. The polypoid stage is either insignificant or lacking.

The anthozoa are cnidarians in which only a polyp stage is present. They include the anemones and the corals and may be solitary or colonial. Cold water corals have soft bodies and do not build the reefs typical of tropical corals.

Whichever shape they exhibit, all the cnidarians produce a unique structure called a nematocyst. This is the part responsible for the notorious sting of the Portuguese Man-of-War. Most cnidarian nematocysts are too weak to affect human skin, however. The nematocyst is a small capsule with a thread-like tube coiled inside. When a trigger bristle is disturbed, the coiled tube shoots out and imbeds in whatever triggered it. There a minute amount of poison is injected. The nematocysts are used for both defense and capturing food.

LEFT Moon Jellyfish, *Aurelia aurita*. This beautiful jellyfish grows to about ten inches across and is found throughout the oceans of the world. It is easily identified by the four horseshoe-shaped gonads. Its tentacles are short and very numerous.

OPPOSITE PAGE This view into the interior of a Moon Jellyfish reveals a small, reddish crustacean. This is the parasitic amphipod *Hyperia galba*. Another amphipod of the same genus parasitizes the Lion's Mane Jellyfish.

Moon Jellyfish and a parasitic Amphipod, *Aurelia aurita* and *Hyperia galba*

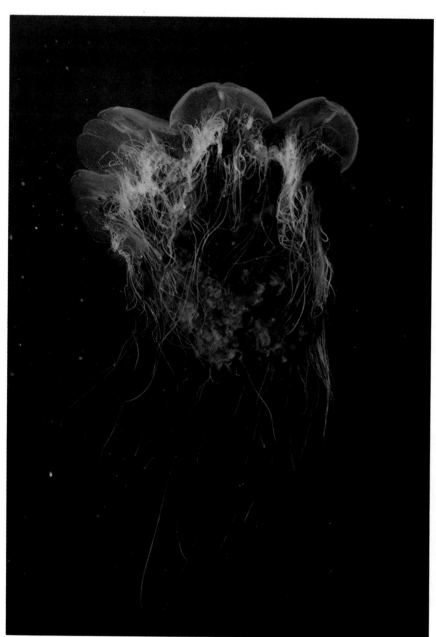

LEFT Lion's Mane Jellyfish, *Cyanea capillata*. This is the largest species of jellyfish in the world. A few, rare individuals reach a diameter of over eight feet across, but most are less than a foot across. A brown muscular mass that hangs below the eight-lobed umbrella gives the Lion's Mane its name. The tentacles of the Lion's Mane have numerous nematocysts that are capable of stinging a swimmer severely.

BELOW Many-Ribbed Jellyfish, *Aequorae sp.* There are several similar species of this beautiful medusae. It may reach a size of over eight inches across.

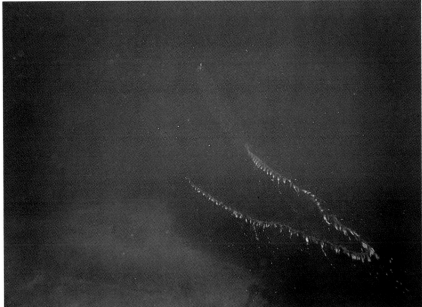

ABOVE   Siphonophore, *Stephanomia sp.* These are extraordinary hydrozoan ocean plankters. They are very unusual colonial animals in which the individuals making up the colony have become greatly differentiated. Different groups of the individual units perform different functions of flotation, locomotion, feeding, and reproduction. The best known siphonophore is the Portuguese Man-of-War.

LEFT   Stalked Jellyfish, *Lucernaria quadricornis.* These small medusae do not resemble the typical jellyfish. They attach themselves to a rock or seaweed by an adhesive pad at the end of their stalk. There are several species in New England. This one, the largest, grows to several inches in length.

LEFT Dead Man's Fingers Soft Coral, *Alcyonium digitatum.* This is a small coral polyp that is quite abundant in New England. It is found growing on rocks and pilings in shallow water. When the animal is disturbed, it withdraws its eight-armed tentacles, leaving only pale fleshy lobes that give it the name Dead Man's Fingers.

OPPOSITE PAGE Branching Soft Coral, *Geresemia rubiformis.* The branching soft coral grows to six or more inches in height. The various species range from a pale flesh color to a rich red. These corals are usually found at depths of sixty feet or more.

Branching Soft Coral, *Bersemia rubiformis.*

LEFT   Northern Red Anemone, *Tealia felina*. This anemone frequently reaches a size of over six inches across. Its thicker tentacles enable it to catch much larger prey than the frilled anemone. Captured food is then drawn into the large mouth that the tentacles encircle. While usually red, this anemone is variable in color. It is usually found in colder waters or depths of thirty feet or more.

OPPOSITE PAGE   The Northern Red Anemone shown here is eating a Many-Ribbed Jellyfish.

Northern Red Anemone and a Many-Ribbed Jellyfish, *Tealia felina* and *Aequorea sp.*

Frilled Sea Anemone, *Metridium senile*

OPPOSITE PAGE   Frilled Sea Anemone, *Metridium senile.* The most common of the sea anemones in the Northeast, the frilled anemone is found on a wide variety of hard substrates from just a few feet below low tide downward. Hundreds of fine tentacles armed with nematocysts catch the small plankton the anemone eats. The frilled anemone can occur in a wide variety of colors and grows to over a foot in height.

RIGHT   This Frilled Anemone is reproducing asexually by budding another anemone off its base.

FOLLOWING SPREAD LEFT   Tiny Frilled Anemones, *Metridium senile* growing among Blue Mussels, *Mytilus edulis.*

FOLLOWING SPREAD RIGHT   Tube Anemone, *Cerianthus borealis.* This anemone lives with its body buried and only its mouth and tentacles showing. If disturbed it will rapidly withdraw into its hole. It has two distinct whorls of tentacles that may be up to eight inches across. It is found at moderate depths where the bottom is soft enough for it to burrow.

Frilled Sea Anemones and Blue Mussels, *Metridium senile* and *Mytilus edulis*

Tube Anemone, *Cerianthus borealis*

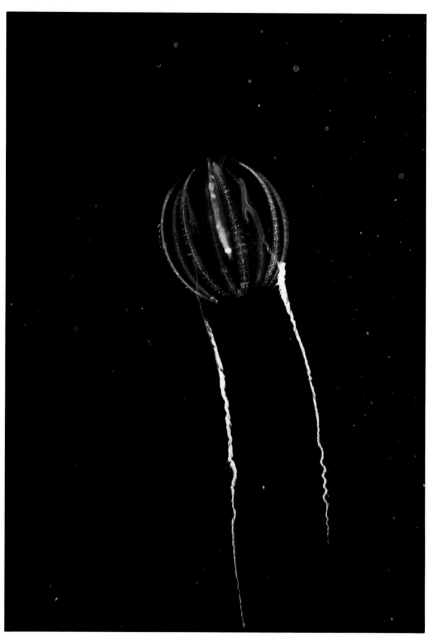

COMB JELLIES:
Phylum Ctenophora

THE COMB JELLIES with their transparent, gelatinous bodies resemble the jellyfish. But they lack both the sessile polypoid stage of many jellyfish and the nematocysts that all cnidarians possess. Most comb jellies have eight rows of comb-like plates covered with fine hairs that give the phylum its name. These are beaten in the water to provide locomotion. This locomotion is too weak to fight prevailing currents in which they drift, so they are members of the planktonic community.

Like many other planktonic animals, they occur in swarms. They are voracious predators of other plankters, sometimes even eating each other. Some have tentacles with which they capture prey. When they occur in large numbers they may sweep the water almost clean of smaller creatures. They, in turn, are eaten by many fish.

LEFT Sea Gooseberry, *Pleurobranchia pileus.* This is a common comb jelly in northern waters. Its spherical body reaches a diameter of about an inch and has two long retractile tentacles.

ABOVE   Beroe's Comb Jelly, *Beroe cucumis.* This comb jelly has a flattened sac-like body with no lobes or tentacles. Mature individuals reach a size of about four inches.

RIGHT   A small Lion's Mane Jellyfish has captured a Beroe's Comb Jelly.

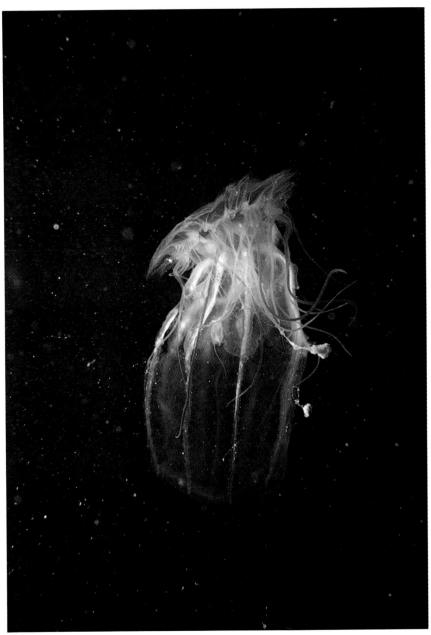

MARINE WORMS

THERE ARE ACTUALLY a number of different phyla of marine worms, based on external or internal structure. Most marine worms burrow in soft bottom sediments or live as parasites inside other animals. This is certainly in part due to the fact that their soft bodies make them easy prey for any larger animal that might catch them in the open. Because of this, there are few marine worms pictured here, even though they are actually very abundant.

Most of the commonly seen marine worms are segmented worms of the phylum Annelida, and are members of the class of bristle worms called polychaetes. The polychaetes are sometimes divided by their behavior into errant polychaetes and sedentary polychaetes. The errant polychaetes are predatory carnivores that rove about in search of prey to capture and eat while the sedentary polychaetes spend their lives in protective tubes and eat the plankton and detritus that are filtered from the sea water.

LEFT Plankton Worm, *Tomopteris helgolandica.* This is a small, transparent polychaete worm that spends its life swimming in the water column. It reaches a length of about three inches.

OPPOSITE Clam Worm, *Nereis virens.* The Clam Worm is a typical predatory polychaete worm. Large individuals reach a length of several feet and prey on a wide variety of other invertebrates. They in turn are eaten by many bottom fish and large crustaceans. They are frequently sold as bait.

Clam Worm, *Nereis virens*

OPPOSITE PAGE Fan Worm, *Myxicola infundibulum*. This is a sedentary polychaete worm of the family of worms called Sabellid worms. These worms live in a tough, leathery, mucus tube they secrete. The worm exposes only its head, which has a circlet of tentacles that have both a feeding and respiratory function. If disturbed, the fan worm withdraws rapidly into its tube.

LEFT Scale Worm, *Lepidonotus squamata*. The scale worm is another polychaete worm that is found abundantly in shallow water. It reaches a length of two inches. Scale worms can often be found under rocks at low tide.

Other phyla of marine worms include the flatworms of the phylum Platyhelmenthes and the ribbon worms of the phylum Nemertea. These worms and others are important for the roles they play as predators and prey in ecological food chains.

Fan Worm, *Myxicola infundibulum*

Hard Tube Worm, *Filograna implexa*

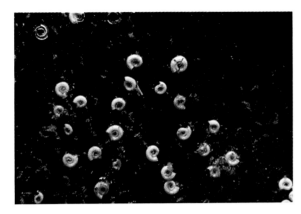

ABOVE Coil Worm, *Spirorbis borealis*. The coil worm is another Serpulid worm. Its tiny calcareous tubes are frequently found on seaweeds. About an eighth of an inch across, the coils of this species all turn counterclockwise. Another almost identical species has tubes with a clockwise turn.

RIGHT Many-Eyed Ribbon Worm, *Amphiporus angulatus*. This worm is an example of a ribbon or nemertean worm. This species grows to a length of about six inches. It lives in shallow water and feeds on small amphipods.

OPPOSITE PAGE Hard Tube Worm, *Filograna implexa*. Colonies of this worm build a twisting network of hard, calcareous tubes that they live in. Worms that build calcareous, rather than mucous, tubes are called Serpulid worms. The brittle calcareous colonies of Filograna are often over a foot across. A small sculpin is hiding beneath this colony.

ECTOPROCTS:
Phylum Ectoprocta

ECTOPROCTS, SOMETIMES CALLED BRYOZOANS or moss animals, are minute, colonial animals that are sessile and live permanently attached to hard substrates. They are frequently found growing on rocks, shells, wharf pilings, and plants. Some colonies are flat and encrusting in nature while others are erect and branching or bushy.

Each colony is composed of minute individual units that require microscopic examination to be seen clearly. Each unit, usually about a half millimeter in size, consists of an animal, called a zooid, and its exoskeleton. Each individual has a mouth surrounded by a circlet of tentacles with which it snares planktonic food.

There are many different species of ectoprocts in New England waters.

ABOVE Sea Lace, *Electra pilosa*. Also called Lacy Crust, this is one of a number of very similar species of colonial, encrusting bryozoans. Various species are found on rocks, shells, seaweeds, almost everywhere.

LEFT Bushy Bugula, *Bugula turrita*. This bryozoan forms dense, branching colonies ranging in color from whitish to orange. Usually only several inches in size, they occasionally reach a foot in height. Another name for this animal is the Tufted Bryozoan.

ABOVE Northern Lamp Shell, *Terebratulina septentrionalis*. The Northern Lamp Shell is the only common shallow-water brachiopod. Its internal structure of circlets of filaments, called lophophores, easily distinguish it from bivalve mollusks which it externally resembles. This brachiopod has a thin layer of the yellow encrusting sponge, *Iophon nigricans*.

LAMP SHELLS:
Phylum Brachiopoda

THE BRACHIOPODS SUPERFICIALLY RESEMBLE small bivalve mollusks, but the shells are hinged dorsally and ventrally instead of laterally. There is also a fleshy stalk-like pedicle which attaches the lampshell to the substrate. The internal structures are also considerably different from those of the mollusks.

Lamp shells are of particular importance in the fossil record of the oceans. During their peak in the Devonian era about 400 million years ago there were over two hundred genera. Today there are only a few remaining, and only one species is commonly found in shallow water in the Gulf of Maine.

This species, the northern lamp shell, *Terebratulina septentrionalis*, is usually found on the sides of rocks among other encrusting animals like bryozoans and tunicates. It, in turn, is frequently covered by an encrusting sponge, *Iophon nigricans*, which is only found on these lamp shells.

MOLLUSKS: Phylum Mollusca

THE MOLLUSKS ARE a large and important phylum that is abundantly represented in the New England area. A number of its members are important food products. These include the clams, mussels, and scallops.

Several very distinctive structural features are found only in the mollusks. One of these is the mantle, a fold in the body wall that secretes the calcium carbonate shell that is typical of mollusks. Another molluscan structure is the radula, a toothed, tongue-like organ that many of the predatory mollusks use to bore through the shells of their prey. A third important structure is the foot, a sole-like creeping structure found in chitons, bivalves, and snails. Many of the mollusks lack one or another of these distinctive structures.

The phylum is divided into six classes of which four are of major importance. These are the Polyplacophora, the Gastropoda, the Bivalvia, and the Cephalopoda.

The Polyplacophora, or chitons, are considered to be the most primitive form of mollusk. Chitons have an oval body covered by a shell composed of eight plates called valves. The chiton holds firmly to the substrate with a typical molluscan foot. Chitons have radular mouth parts and feed on algae and other vegetation.

The class Gastropoda is the largest and most diverse of the

LEFT Waved Whelk, *Buccinum undatum.*

Red Chiton, *Ischnochiton ruber*. The red chiton is frequently found in shallow water clinging to the sides of rocks. It reaches a size of about an inch.

Tortoiseshell Limpet, *Acmaea testudinalis*. This inch-long mollusk is found abundantly on rocks in the intertidal zone and in shallow waters.

classes. The soft body has an easily distinguished head, mantle, foot, and visceral mass. The head is the center of the sensory organs, usually having eyes and tentacles. The mouth with radular parts is also located on the head. The typical gastropod shell is a single spiral-shaped cone. Most have a right-handed direction to the spiral. The foot of the snail often has a plate called an operculum that covers the opening of the shell when the animal withdraws into the shell.

A number of gastropods have no shell. Many of these are sea slugs, also called nudibranchs. Some nudibranchs that feed on cnidarians are able to ingest the nematocysts without discharging them. They then use the nematocysts for their own defense.

Members of the class Bivalvia are easily recognized because their shells have two halves, called valves. The two valves are joined by a hinge and controlled by one or two adductor muscles. Many of the bivalves are important commercial food products. Clams, oysters, mussels, and scallops are all highly edible. While most gastropods are scavengers or predators, the typical bivalve is a filter feeder of plankton. Sea water is drawn in and exhaled through siphons. In the case of clams, which live buried in sand or mud, all that protrudes above the surface of the bottom is the siphons. Mussels are found attached to a solid substrate like rocks or pilings.

The class Cephalopoda includes the squids and octopi. These seemingly intelligent animals are among the most highly evolved invertebrates. Both squid and octopi have arms with numerous suction discs for grasping prey. Both are also capable of rapid changes in coloration. The New England species of octopus is a deep-water animal and is rarely seen by divers. Squid are sometimes seen inshore at night where they pursue small fish such as herring.

LEFT Waved Whelk, *Buccinum undatum.* The waved whelk is one of the major predatory whelks of the rocky shores of the Gulf of Maine. It is also the edible whelk that is eaten in Europe. This whelk commonly feeds on mussels and other invertebrates, but will scavenge on dead fish. Lobstermen consider it a bait stealer. The waved whelk reaches a length of about three inches. This whelk is laying eggs on the side of a rock.

OPPOSITE PAGE This Waved Whelk is eating a sea urchin that has been broken open.

Waved Whelk and a Green Sea Urchin, *Buccinum undatum* and *Strongylcentrotus droebachiensis*

Northern Moon Snail, *Lunatia heros*

ABOVE   A sand collar, the egg case of the moon snail.

OPPOSITE PAGE   Northern Moon Snail, *Lunatia heros*. Another predatory gastropod, the moon snail inhabits the areas of sandy or muddy bottoms where it preys on clams and other bivalves. The moon snail lays its eggs in a mucous sand case called a sand collar.

ABOVE   Common Periwinkle, *Littorina littorea*. This snail is abundant along rocky shores. About an inch in size, it feeds on algae. It is frequently found covering rocks in the intertidal zone and in tide pools. There are several different species in New England waters.

FOLLOWING SPREAD LEFT   Stimpson's Whelk, *Colus stimpsoni*. Stimpson's whelk is found on the sand and mud bottomed regions. It reaches a length of five inches.

FOLLOWING SPREAD RIGHT   Naked Sea Butterfly, *Clione limacina*. This beautiful mollusk is a free-swimming, shell-less gastropod. They grow to a length of about one inch. Sea butterflies are usually found offshore where they may occur in such large schools that they become an important food for whales.

Stimpson's Whelk, *Colus stimpsoni*

Naked Sea Butterfly, *Clione limacina*

Maned Nudibranch, *Aeolidia papillosa*

Red-Gilled Nudibranch, *Coryphella verrucosa*

Rough-Mantled Nudibranch, *Onchidoris bilamellata*

ABOVE   This is a completed egg veil of the rough-mantled nudibranch.

OPPOSITE PAGE   Rough-Mantled Nudibranch, *Onchidoris bilamellata*. These inch-long nudibranchs are laying eggs. The rough-mantled nudibranch eats barnacles and is very often found on bridge and dock pilings where barnacles are abundant.

RIGHT ABOVE   Sponge-Eating Nudibranch, *Cadlina Laevis*. Cadlina grows to about an inch in size. It is usually found on or near the flat encrusting sponge *Halisarca sp.,* its preferred food.

RIGHT BELOW   Rim-Backed Nudibranch, *Polycera dubia*. This tiny green sea slug is usually found among ectoprocts. It grows to about a half inch in length.

PRECEDING SPREAD LEFT   Maned Nudibranch, *Aeolidia papillosa*. This shell-less gastropod is one of the larger nudibranchs in New England waters. It feeds on anemones and reaches a length of four inches.

PRECEDING SPREAD RIGHT   Red-Gilled Nudibranch, *Coryphella verrucosa*. This inch-long nudibranch is often abundant in areas with the Tubularian hydroids on which it feeds.

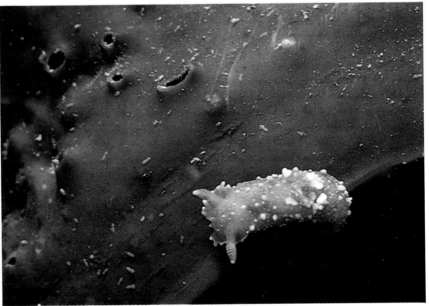

Blue Mussel, *Mytilus edulis*

OPPOSITE PAGE Blue Mussel, *Mytilus edulis*. This is the common edible mussel. It is found abundantly in shallow water on almost any solid substrate. It grows to a length of four inches but is frequently less, especially where dense populations have stunted growth.

RIGHT Horse Mussel, *Modiolus modiolus*. This mussel is often found in the same waters as the Blue Mussel, but at slightly greater depths, usually below thirty feet. It is edible, but has a flavor many find too strong. It grows to a length of six inches.

LEFT Deep-Sea Scallop, *Placopecten magellanicus.* This scallop, the largest of several species in New England, grows to over eight inches across. It is usually found on mud bottoms from depths just below low tide downward.

OPPOSITE PAGE Iceland Scallop, *Chalmys islandica.* The Iceland Scallop is found in the northern portions of the Gulf of Maine. Like the other species of scallop, it has a row of many small eyes at the very edge of its mantle. The Iceland Scallop reaches a size of four inches.

Iceland Scallop, *Chalmys islandica*

THIS SPREAD Boreal Squid, *Illex illecebrosus.* The boreal squid is commonly found in the Gulf of Maine. It has ten tentacles and reaches a length of about fifteen inches. It is frequently found inshore at night in the late summer chasing small fish, and sometimes grounds itself in the pursuit.

Boreal Squid, *Illex illecebrosus*

ARTHROPODS:
Phylum Arthropoda

THE PHYLUM ARTHROPODA is the largest phylum of the animal kingdom. With its insect hordes and myriads of crustaceans it has twice as many species as the next largest phylum, the mollusks. The major characteristic of the Arthropods is their jointed, armor-like, exoskeleton. With a few exceptions that include the sea spiders, horseshoe crabs, mites, and some insects, most of the marine arthropods fall in the class Crustacea. The crustaceans include the crabs, shrimp, and lobsters. They also include many small planktonic animals that are significant parts of marine food chains, such as copepods and krill.

Commercially important crustaceans include shrimp, crabs, and most important, the lobster. Various species of each are fished for in New England waters.

The typical crustacean body is composed of a head, a thorax, and an abdomen. In the higher crustaceans there are nineteen body segments, each of which may have a pair of jointed appendages.

LEFT   Acadian Hermit Crab, *Pagurus acadianus.*

OPPOSITE PAGE   Northern Rock Barnacle, *Balanus balanoides.* This small barnacle is found abundantly in the intertidal zone. It reaches a maximum size of about an inch. The tiny animal within the shell filters plankton from the water with six pairs of cirri.

Northern Rock Barnacle, *Balanus balanoides*

THIS SPREAD American Lobster, *Homarus americanus*. The American lobster is the seafood delicacy most associated with the New England coast. The largest lobsters reach a size of over three feet in length and over forty-five pounds. They eat a wide variety of fish and invertebrates, including other lobsters.

Crustaceans grow by shedding their hard exoskeletons when they become too tight. The old shell usually splits along the upper surface and the animal backs out. The process is called molting and is a period of particular danger for the animal as it lacks protective armor until lime salts are deposited to form a new skeleton. During this time, which may last for weeks, the animal is virtually defenseless and frequently hides in crevices.

Arthropods reproduce sexually. In some cases the female can mate only immediately after she has molted. Many of the crustaceans have planktonic larval stages that provide a wide dispersal for the young.

American Lobster, *Homarus americanus*

Caridean Shrimp, *Lebbeus groenlandicus*

Montague's Shrimp, *Pandalus montagui*

PRECEDING SPREAD LEFT   Caridean Shrimp, *Lebbeus groenlandicus.* This heavy-bodied shrimp is found in the northern portions of the Gulf of Maine. It reaches a length of more than two inches.

PRECEDING SPREAD RIGHT   Montague's Shrimp, *Pandalus montagui.* Montague's shrimp is one of several species that are the native pink shrimp that are commercially fished in New England. They are normally found at depths below a hundred feet, except in the northernmost parts of the Gulf of Maine.

OPPOSITE PAGE   Toad Crab, *Hyas coarctatus.* This is a shallow water species of spider crab. Many toad crabs encourage sponges and other encrusting animals to grow on their shells. This serves to help camouflage the toad crab and also has given it the name decorator crab.

LEFT   Caprellid Amphipod, *Caprella sp.* Sometimes called skeleton shrimp, these tiny crustaceans resemble a little preying mantis. They are found among the finer seaweeds where they cling to the vegetation with their hind legs and grab tiny bits of food with their claws. Most caprellids are less than an inch long.

BELOW   Mysid Shrimp, *Mysis sp.* Mysid shrimp are sometimes called opossum shrimp because they brood their eggs in a pouch. Abundant in many shallow water areas, mysids reach a length of almost two inches. Sometimes in the spring the shallows are alive with clouds of freshly hatched mysid shrimp.

Toad Crab, *Hyas coarctatus*

Rock Crab, *Cancer irroratus*

ABOVE   These Rock Crabs are mating. Mating can occur only during a brief time after the female has shed her old shell and before her new one has hardened.

RIGHT   Rock Crab, *Cancer irroratus*. The Rock Crab is one of the most common crabs in New England. It is found intertidally and downward to depths of over two thousand feet. Large individuals reach a size of about five inches across the carapace.

OPPOSITE PAGE   Rock Crabs often eat sea urchins as well as small crustaceans and mollusks.

Acadian Hermit Crab, *Pagurus acadianus*

ABOVE   Hairy Hermit Crab, *Pagurus arcuatus.* The Hairy Hermit Crab is usually found in deeper, colder water than the Acadian Hermit Crab. Similar in size, its claws are covered with a thick growth of hairs.

FOLLOWING SPREAD LEFT   Anemone Sea Spider, *Pycnogonum littorale.* This sea spider is found on the Frilled Sea Anemone, which it parasitizes. Digging its claws into the anemone, it pushes its proboscis through the anemone's skin and sucks out body juices. It reaches a size of over an inch across.

FOLLOWING SPREAD RIGHT   Atlantic Horseshoe Crab, *Limulus polyphemus.* The ancient ancestors of the horseshoe crab lived in the Devonian seas over 350 million years ago. This unusual arthropod is really more closely related to spiders and other arachnids than to crabs and crustaceans. It is found in the southern parts of the Gulf of Maine and reaches a length of two feet.

OPPOSITE PAGE   Acadian Hermit Crab, *Pagurus acadianus.* Herbit Crabs have the distinctive habit of using empty gastropod shells as their home. The Acadian Hermit Crab is one of the more common large Hermit Crabs in the Gulf of Maine. They frequently use the shells of the waved whelk or moon snail.

Anemone Sea Spider, *Pycnogonum littorale*

Atlantic Horseshoe Crab, *Limulus polyphemus*

SPINY-SKINNED ANIMALS:
Phylum Echinodermata

THE ECHINODERMS GET THEIR NAME from the fact that their basic skeletal structure is a network of calcareous plates with spines embedded in the skin. Different groups within the phylum have these plates in different degrees. In the sea urchins the plates are so closely locked together that they form an immovable, rigid shell. In the brittle stars and sea stars the plates articulate with each other and allow a considerable degree of flexibility and movement. In the sea cucumbers the plates are so loosely scattered that the skin appears soft and leathery.

The echinoderms also share several other characteristics. They have bodies that are based on a five-part radial pattern of symmetry. They also possess an internal water-vascular system. The tube feet used for locomotion by most of the echinoderms are part of this water-vascular system.

The three major classes of the echinoderms are the Holothuroidea or sea cucumbers, the Echinoidea or sea urchins and sand dollars, and the Stellaroidea or stars. The Stellaroidea is divided into two major subclasses, the sea stars and the brittle stars.

LEFT   Northern Basket Star, *Gorgonocephalus arcticus.*

OPPOSITE PAGE   Purple Sea Star, *Asterias vulgaris.* The Purple Sea Star is the most common shallow water sea star in the Gulf of Maine. Large specimens reach over a foot across.

Purple Sea Star, *Asterias vulgaris*

ABOVE   Tube feet of the purple sea star.

RIGHT   Purple Sea Star, *Asterias vulgaris*. This sea star is draped over a mussel, which it will open by pulling on the two halves of the shell until the mussel tires. The star will then push its stomach out the opening on its underside and into the mussel's shell where it will digest the soft body of the mussel.

OPPOSITE PAGE   Blood Star, *Henricia sanguinolenta*. This is another sea star that can be found in shallow water. Though this one is purple, it may be yellow, red, or even flesh colored. It feeds on sponges.

Blood Star, *Henricia sanguinolenta*

Spiny Sunstar, *Crossaster papposus*

OPPOSITE PAGE   Spiny Sunstar, *Crossaster papposus.* This bright-red many-armed sea star is usually found in deeper, colder waters of sixty feet or more. It frequently has bold concentric patterns of pink or white and reaches a size of almost a foot across. It eats other sea stars.

RIGHT   Purple Sunstar, *Solaster endeca.* The purple sunstar is another star that is usually found in deeper water. It is frequently a foot across. Solaster feeds on sea cucumbers.

Red Gold-Bordered Sea Star, *Hippasteria phrygiana*

Sponge-Eating Sea Star, *Pteraster militaris*

LEFT   Daisy Brittle Star, *Ophiopholis aculeata*. This is the most common brittle star in our shallow waters. It is found abundantly under rocks, among mussels, and entwined in the holdfasts of kelp. It reaches a diameter of over eight inches.

OPPOSITE PAGE   Northern Basket Star, *Gorgonocephalus arcticus*. This unusual star is a member of the brittle stars. It is relatively rare in the Gulf of Maine south of the Bay of Fundy, but there it is quite numerous in spots where many basket stars may be found spreading their branching arms in the current to snare bits of food. Large specimens have an arm spread of well over a foot.

BELOW   Young basket stars are often found parasitizing soft corals.

PRECEDING SPREAD LEFT   Red Gold-Bordered Sea Star, *Hippasteria phrygiana*. This large, stout sea star feeds on soft corals. It is frequently found on muddy bottoms at depths of sixty feet or more. It is often more than a foot across.

PRECEDING SPREAD RIGHT   Sponge-Eating Sea Star, *Pteraster militaris*. This star reaches a size of about six inches. It has the unusual characteristic of brooding its young under a membrane that covers the dorsal surface, rather than bearing free-swimming planktonic larvae as in many stars. When they are released, the tiny stars resemble their parents.

Northern Basket Star, *Gorgonocephalus arcticus*

Green Sea Urchin, *Strongylocentrotus droebachiensis*

ABOVE AND OPPOSITE PAGE   Green Sea Urchin, *Strongylocentrotus droebachiensis*. The green sea urchin is found abundantly in many areas from just below the low tide mark downward to considerable depths. It reaches a diameter of about three inches.

RIGHT   Sand Dollar, *Echinarachnius parma*. Sand Dollars are found in areas of sandy bottoms where they push across the loose sand, eating diatoms and other micro organisms. They range in color from dark brown to red and reach a diameter of three inches.

LEFT   Scarlet Psolus, *Psolus fabricii*. This is a much smaller sea cucumber than the more common orange-footed variety. It is usually found in deeper, colder water where it clings to the sides of rocks. Large specimens reach a size of eight inches, but most are about the size of an egg.

OPPOSITE PAGE   Orange-Footed Sea Cucumber, *Cucumaria frondosa*. This animal has a brown leathery body with five bands of tube feet. It also has ten retractile tentacles that it uses to capture plankton. As it feeds, the sea cucumber pushes one tentacle after another into its mouth to strip off the plankton. This species of sea cucumber reaches a length of almost two feet.

Orange-Footed Sea Cucumber, *Cucumaria frondosa*

TUNICATES: Phylum Chordata

THE TUNICATES ARE a rather large but unimpressive-looking group of animals. Their main claim to fame is the fact that among all the invertebrates, they are most closely akin to the vertebrates. This is because at some time during their life cycle they possess gill slits, a dorsal nerve cord, and a structure called a notochord. The notochord is a rod-like supporting structure that is the forerunner of the vertebral column. These features, with the exception of gill slits, are usually present only during a tadpole-shaped larval stage and degenerate in the adult.

The name tunicate comes from the tough external covering or tunic of the adult animal. The adult tunicate usually has two openings, an incurrent, branchial siphon and an excurrent, atrial siphon. The tunicate filters sea water for plankton and detritus. There are both colonial and individual species of tunicates.

LEFT Stalked Ascidians, *Boltenia ovifera.* This unmistakable tunicate is found subtidally downward to considerable depths. The body reaches a size of three inches and grows atop a stalk several times the length of the body.

OPPOSITE PAGE White Crust, *Didemnum candidum.* This is a flat colonial tunicate made up of many small individuals. The colonies often reach a length of several inches. They are common at the low end of the intertidal zone and in the shallow waters below.

White Crust, *Didemnum candidum*

ABOVE   Sea Peach, *Halocynthia pyriformis*. The Sea Peach is commonly found in shallow water attached to rocks and other solid substrates. While usually orange-red in color, some individuals are much paler. The two siphons are large and obvious, but may be contracted if the animal is disturbed. It frequently reaches a size of several inches across.

RIGHT   Sea Grapes, *Mogula manhattensis*. This is one of a number of small sea squirts called Sea Grapes. Most are found encrusting rocks and pilings in shallow waters, often themselves encrusted by bryozoans. Most Sea Grapes are less than an inch across. Dissection is necessary to determine the exact species.

OPPOSITE PAGE   Sea Vase, *Ciona intestinalis*. This slender sea squirt reaches a length of over three inches. It is found between rocks and attached to pilings.

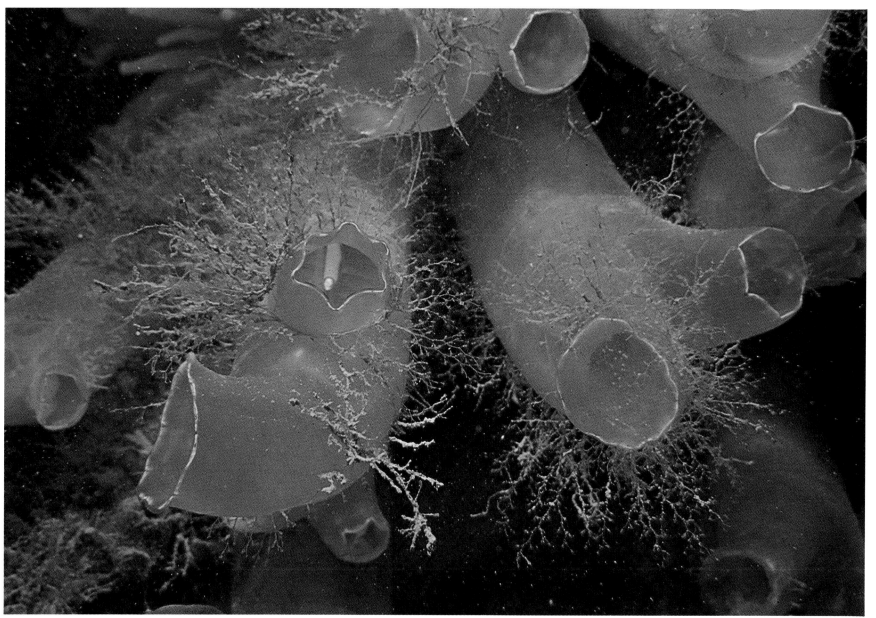

Sea Vase, *Ciona intestinalis*

FISH: Phylum Chordata

THE FISH ARE not a phylum of their own, but instead occupy several classes within the phylum Chordata, along with the classes of tunicates, birds, mammals, and other animals with backbones.

There are a number of characteristics that are common to most fish. They all have a backbone. They breathe by removing oxygen from the water using gills. They possess fins, either paired or unpaired, which are used for locomotion and stability in the water.

There are three classes of fish. The first and most primitive is the Class Agnatha. This class includes the lampreys and hagfish. They have a backbone of cartilage rather than true bone, have no true jaws, and have no paired fins or scales. They are eel-like in appearance and have a jawless mouth with sucking parts.

The second class of fish is the Class Chondrichthyes. This class includes the sharks and the rays. These fish also have a skeleton of cartilage, but they also have true jaws, scales and paired fins.

The third and largest class of fish is the Class Osteichthyes. These are the bony fish with skeletons of bone rather than cartilage.

The fish have demonstrated a wide range of adaptation to their

LEFT   Schooling Pollock, *Pollachius virens.*

OPPOSITE PAGE   Big Skate and Winter Flounder, *Raja ocellata* and *Pseudopleuronectes americanus.*

Big Skate and a Winter Flounder, *Raja ocellata* and *Pseudopleuronectes americanus*

LEFT Spiny Dogfish, *Squalus acanthias*. The spiny dogfish is by far the most common shark in the Gulf of Maine. Often schooling in huge numbers, they devour and drive off other species of fish. Adult dogfish reach a length of about three feet.

particular environments. The fast-swimming fish have the streamlined teardrop shape and have coverings of scales to further reduce the water's drag. Many of these pelagic or free-swimming fish have a dark-above, light-below coloration pattern that makes them less visible to predators. These same fish often swim in schools which may protect individuals from predators.

The fish that live on the oceans' floor have undergone an even wider range of adaptation. Many of those that live on the vast flat sandy regions have become flat themselves. Among these are the rays and the flounders. Another adaptive shape is the eel-shaped body of fish that live among the rocks and crevices. This shape allows them to get into cracks and holes in search of food or for protection. Still other fish have modified fins that are used to feel around or even attract prey.

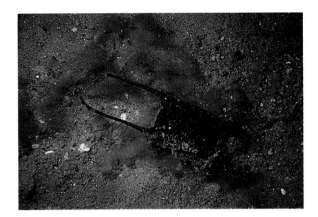

ABOVE   A skate egg case.

RIGHT   Big Skate, *Raja ocellata*. The big skate is one of about half a dozen species of skate found in the Gulf of Maine. The big skate reaches a length of about three and a half feet. Skates spend most of their time close to the bottom, often partially buried in the sand or mud. They feed on a wide variety of crustaceans and smaller fish. Skates lay their eggs in dark, oblong, leathery cases that are sometimes washed ashore after storms.

Quite a few of the several hundred species of fish in the Gulf of Maine are edible and are the basis for a large fishing industry. Fish are also very significant within the marine ecosystem as they are predators of major significance at the top of the food chains.

FOLLOWING SPREAD LEFT   Herring, *Clupea harengus*. The herring is the basis for an active commercial fishery in the Gulf of Maine. Immature herring in their first and second years are caught and marketed as sardines. These are four to eight inches long, while the adults reach a length of about a foot and a half. Herring are plankton feeders and often occur in huge schools.

FOLLOWING SPREAD RIGHT   Pollock, *Pollachius virens*. The pollock is a fish commonly found schooling inshore. They reach a length of over three feet, but small fish are more common. They are fished commercially and often sold under the name Boston bluefish.

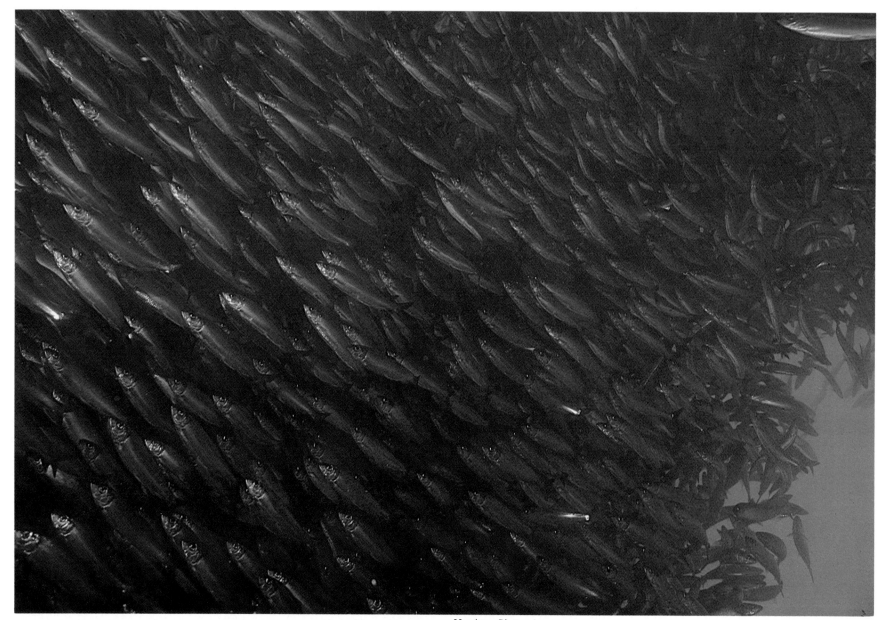

Herring, *Clupea harengus*

Pollock, *Pollachius virens*

LEFT Cod, *Gadus callarias*. The Cod is one of the best known New England fish. It has been commercially important since colonial times. Today the average cod caught weighs about ten pounds, but the record is a six-foot-long fish weighing 211¼ pounds. Cod are bottom feeding fish that are most commonly found on rocky bottomed areas.

ABOVE Black Sea Bass, *Centropristes striatus*. A comparatively infrequent fish in the Gulf of Maine, this fish is an important fish south of Cape Cod. It reaches a size of about two feet.

RIGHT Cunner, *Tautogolabrus adspersus*. The cunner is a shallow water fish found abundantly right up to the low tide mark. They are aggressive scavengers, feeding on a wide variety of small crustaceans, especially amphipods and shrimps, as well as small mollusks, marine worms, and occasional small fish. They are usually six to ten inches in length.

FOLLOWING SPREAD LEFT Rosefish, *Sebastes marinus*. The rosefish, often commercially sold as ocean perch, is most commonly found in colder, deeper waters. Rare individuals reach a length of two feet, but nine to fifteen inches is more usual. It can sometimes be found in shallow waters in the Bay of Fundy region.

FOLLOWING SPREAD RIGHT Squirrel Hake, *Urophycis chuss*. The squirrel hake is a bottom fish found throughout the Gulf of Maine. It forages for food chiefly at night, using its long filamentous ventral fins to detect small crustaceans. They also feed on other smaller fish and squid.

Rosefish, *Sebastes marinus*

Squirrel Hake, *Urophycis chuss*

LEFT Lumpfish, *Cyclopterus lumpus*. This heavy-bodied bottom fish is usually found in offshore waters, but in the spring and early summer it swims into shallow waters to spawn. There the female lays her eggs and returns to deeper water, leaving the male who will guard the eggs and fan them until they hatch. Lumpfish exhibit a wide variety of coloration. They are typically about a foot in length or less, but rare individuals may reach almost twice that.

OPPOSITE PAGE This male lumpfish is guarding the clump of eggs that are behind the green sea urchin to the left of the lumpfish. Some people eat lumpfish eggs as a poor man's caviar.

Lumpfish, *Cyclopterus lumpus*

Winter Flounder, *Pseudopleuronectes americanus*

ABOVE This shot of a winter flounder shows clearly that both eyes are now on what was the right side of the fish, but that the mouth has remained in its original position.

RIGHT This series of three shots shows the remarkable ability of the flounder to change its coloration to match a wide range of bottom colorations.

OPPOSITE PAGE Winter Flounder, *Pseudopleuronectes americanus*. The Winter flounder is one member of a tribe of fine-tasting flatfish that includes the soles, the dabs, and the huge halibut. An unusual early development results in both eyes being situated on one side of the fish, which swims with the other side down. Depending on the species, the eyes may be on what was the right side or the left side. The winter flounder is a species whose eyes are situated on what was originally its right side. Flounders also possess the ability to change their coloration to match the bottom they are on. The Winter flounder is the most common shallow water flounder in the Gulf of Maine. It reaches a length of well over a foot.

THIS SPREAD   Sand Flounder, *Lophopsetta maculata*. The sand flounder is an example of the flounders that are left-sided, that is the eyes and the viscera are on what was originally the left side of the young fish. However this particular flounder has lost an upper eye in some accident. This flounder is so thin that when it is held against the light the body appears somewhat translucent. Because of this it is sometimes called the Windowpane flounder. It is usually under a foot in length.

Sand Flounder, *Lophopsetta maculata*

THIS SPREAD Wolffish, *Anarhichas lupus.* The wolffish possesses one of the most formidable sets of teeth of any fish in the Gulf of Maine, other than the occasional shark. Behind the large canine teeth are large solid molars. With these the wolffish is able to grind open clams and mussels. It also eats sea urchins and various crustaceans. Wolffish sometimes attain a length of five feet and a weight approaching forty pounds.

FOLLOWING SPREAD LEFT Ocean Pout, *Macrozoarces americanus.* The ocean pout is another fish with an eel-like shape. It derives the name pout from its thick lips that give it a pouting countenance. They commonly feed on shelled mollusks, crustaceans, and echinoderms, especially sand dollars. Pouts grow to a length of over three feet and a weight of about ten pounds.

FOLLOWING SPREAD RIGHT Rock Eel, *Pholis gunnellus.* The rock eel is abundant in areas where they can hide among seaweeds or rocky bottoms. Occasionally they can be found stranded in tide pools. The maximum length is about a foot, but most rock eels are less than six inches.

Wolffish, *Anarhichas lupus*

Ocean Pout, *Macrozoarces americanus*

Rock Eel, *Pholis gunnellus*

Longhorn Sculpin, *Myoxocephalus octodecimspinosus*

Shorthorn Sculpin, *Myoxocephalus scorpius*

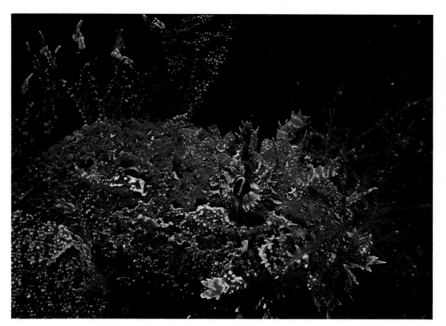

THIS SPREAD Sea Raven, *Hemitripterus americanus*. The Sea Raven is another member of the sculpin family, but has an appearance so distinctive that there can be no confusing it with the other sculpins. It has a ragged first dorsal fin and numerous fleshy tabs on its head. It may be any of a wide range of colors from a dark brown, to brick red, to a bright yellow. When caught or irritated, the sea raven has the curious habit of inflating its belly with water to present an enlarged appearance. It is frequently well over a foot in length.

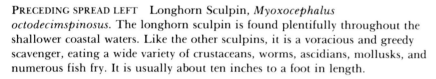

PRECEDING SPREAD LEFT   Longhorn Sculpin, *Myoxocephalus octodecimspinosus*. The longhorn sculpin is found plentifully throughout the shallower coastal waters. Like the other sculpins, it is a voracious and greedy scavenger, eating a wide variety of crustaceans, worms, ascidians, mollusks, and numerous fish fry. It is usually about ten inches to a foot in length.

PRECEDING SPREAD RIGHT   Shorthorn Sculpin, *Myoxocephalus scorpius.* The Shorthorn is the largest of the Gulf of Maine sculpins. It sometimes reaches a length of over two feet, but eight to fourteen inches is the more usual size. It can be easily distinguished from the somewhat smaller longhorn by the length of the uppermost cheek spine. In the shorthorn this spine is less than twice the length of the one below it and reaches only about halfway to the edge of the gill cover. This cheek spine in the longhorn is over four times as long as the one below it and reaches all the way back to the gill-cover edge. The habits and food preferences are the same as those of the longhorn sculpin. This shorthorn is partially encrusted by pink coralline algae which helps him blend in with his surroundings.

118

Sea Raven, *Hemitripterus americanus*

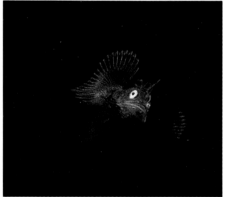

ABOVE   Life for a goosefish begins in a huge floating egg veil that may be up to thirty feet long and have over a million eggs.

ABOVE RIGHT   This juvenile goosefish is barely an inch long. By the time it reaches just over two inches, it will settle to the bottom and begin to flatten out like the adult goosefish.

OPPOSITE PAGE   American Goosefish, *Lophius americanus*. The goosefish is one of the most unusual fish found in the Gulf of Maine. It is one of a group of fish called angler fish. These fish use a fleshy lure to coax their prey close enough to be engulfed with a sudden lunge. The goosefish grows to over four feet in length and over fifty pounds. Like the flounders, the goosefish is able to change its coloration to help it blend in with its surroundings.

American Goosefish, *Lophius americanus*

ABOVE   This adult goosefish has raised its angler.

RIGHT   A close look at the angler clearly shows the leaf-shaped fleshy tab that serves as the goosefish's bait.

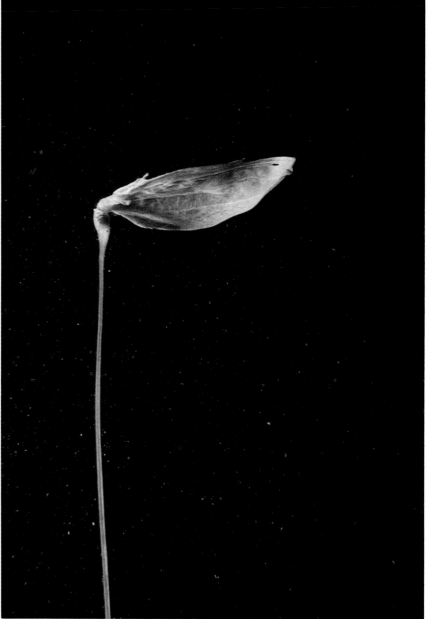

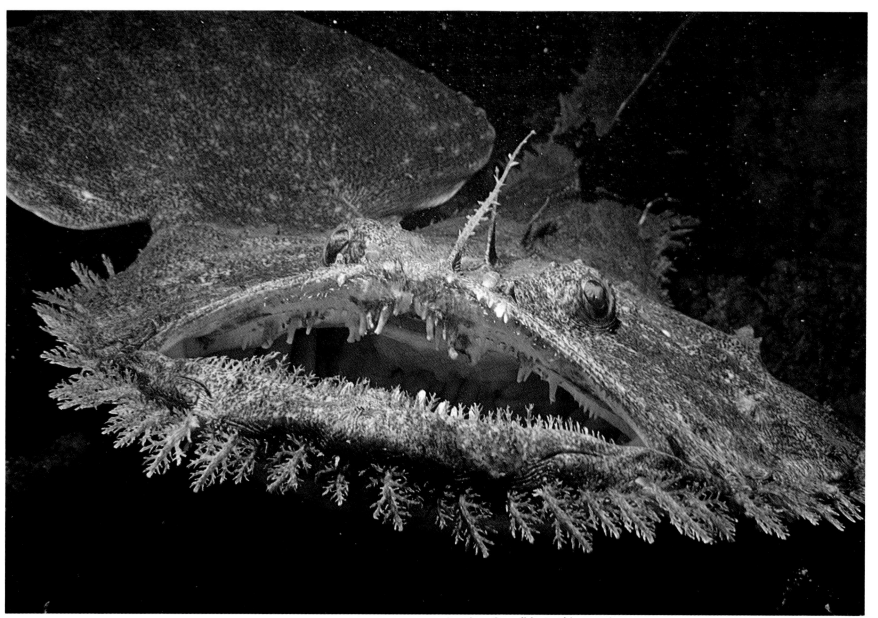

American Goosefish, *Lophius americanus*

Index